Too Many Webs for Anansi

An African-Caribbean tale told by Malachy Doyle

Bc
abc
ww

Illustrated by Lisa Smith

W

FRANKLIN WATTS

First published in 2010 by
Franklin Watts
338 Euston Road
London
NW1 3BH

Franklin Watts Australia
Level 17/207 Kent Street
Sydney
NSW 2000

A CIP catalogue record for this book is available
from the British Library.

ISBN 978 0 7496 9420 3 (hbk)
ISBN 978 0 7496 9426 5 (pbk)

Series Editor: Jackie Hamley
Editor: Melanie Palmer
Series Advisor: Catherine Glavina
Series Designer: Peter Scoulding

Printed in China

To find out more about Malachy
Doyle and his books, please visit:
www.malachydoyle.com

Franklin Watts is a division of
Hachette Children's Books,
an Hachette UK company.
www.hachette.co.uk

This story comes from
West Africa. Can you
find this on a map?

Anansi went to Rabbit's
house. Rabbit was
cooking carrots.

"I love carrots!" said Anansi.

"They're not ready yet,"
said Rabbit.

So Anansi spun a web. He tied one end around his leg and the other to the pot.

"When they're ready, tug on the web and I'll come running," he told Rabbit.

"I smell beans!" cried
Anansi.

"They're not ready yet,"
said Monkey.

But Anansi couldn't wait.
He spun another web, tied
his leg to the bean pot,
and off he went.

13

"Mmm, sweet potatoes!"
cried Anansi.

"They're not ready yet," said Hog. So Anansi spun another web.

By the time Anansi got to the river, he had a web tied to each of his eight legs.

Just then, he felt a tug.
"Carrots!" cried Anansi.

Then he felt another tug.
"Beans!"

21

And then a third tug.
"Sweet potatoes!"

Soon all eight legs were being tugged, this way and that.

"Ouch!" cried Anansi, as his legs were pulled thinner and thinner, longer and longer.

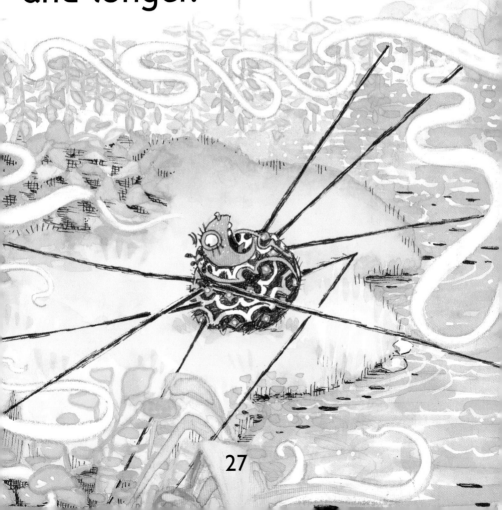

"I was too greedy!" he moaned, rolling into the river to wash all the webs away. "Now I've ended up with nothing!"

Puzzle 1

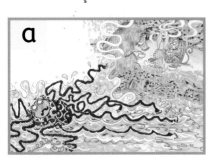

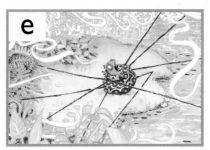

Put these pictures in the correct order.
Now tell the story in your own words.
What different endings can you think of?

greedy   helpful

impatient

kind   sharing

selfish

patient   generous

mean

Choose the correct words for each character. Which words are incorrect? Turn over to find the answers.

Answers

Puzzle 1

The correct order is 1c, 2f, 3b, 4d, 5e, 6a

Puzzle 2

Anansi: the correct words are greedy, impatient

The incorrect word is helpful

Monkey: the correct words are kind, sharing

The incorrect word is selfish

Rabbit: the correct words are generous, patient

The incorrect word is mean

Look out for more Leapfrog World Tales:

Chief Five Heads
ISBN 978 0 7496 8593 5*
ISBN 978 0 7496 8599 7

Baba Yaga
ISBN 978 0 7496 8594 2*
ISBN 978 0 7496 8600 0

Issun Boshi
ISBN 978 0 7496 8595 9*
ISBN 978 0 7496 8601 7

The Frog Emperor
ISBN 978 0 7496 8596 6*
ISBN 978 0 7496 8602 4

The Gold-Giving Snake
ISBN 978 0 7496 8597 3*
ISBN 978 0 7496 8603 1

The Bone Giant
ISBN 978 0 7496 8598 0*
ISBN 978 0 7496 8604 8

Bluebird and Coyote
ISBN 978 0 7496 9415 9*
ISBN 978 0 7496 9421 0

Anansi the Banana Thief
ISBN 978 0 7496 9416 6*
ISBN 978 0 7496 9422 7

Brer Rabbit and the Well
ISBN 978 0 7496 9417 3*
ISBN 978 0 7496 9423 4

Little Tiger and the Fire
ISBN 978 0 7496 9418 0*
ISBN 978 0 7496 9424 1

No Turtle Stew Today
ISBN 978 0 7496 9419 7*
ISBN 978 0 7496 9425 8

Too Many Webs for Anansi
ISBN 978 0 7496 9420 3*
ISBN 978 0 7496 9426 5

*hardback